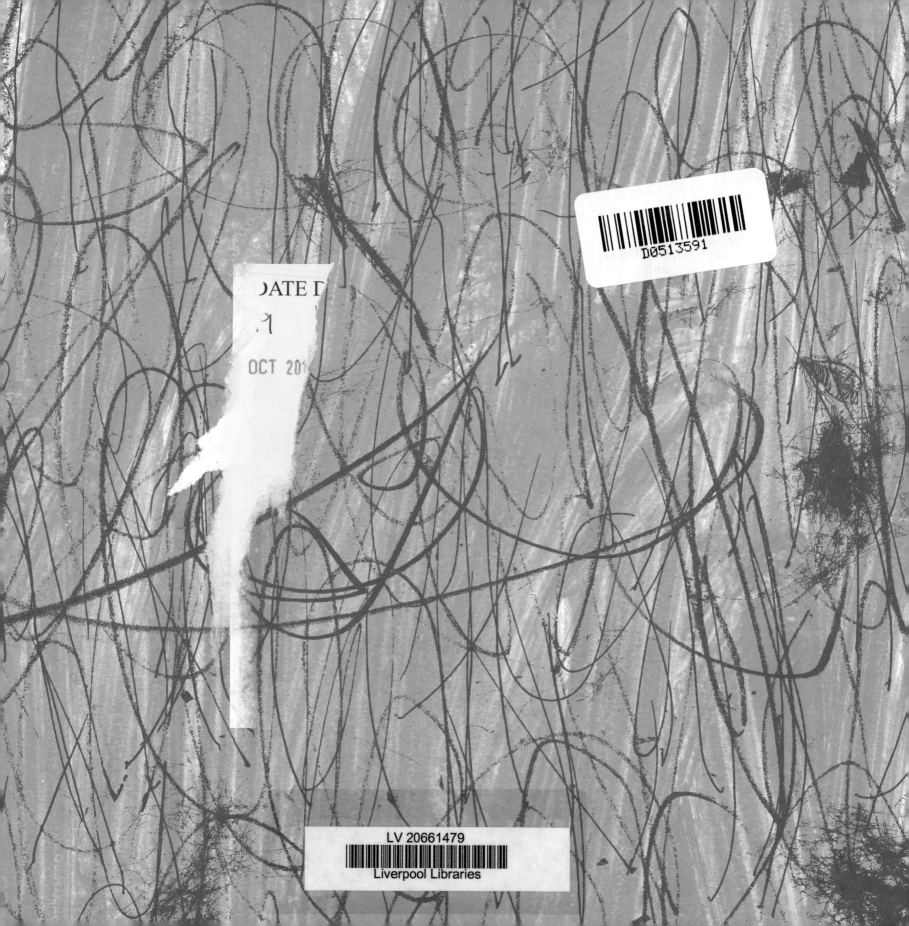

SUN

PLANET EARTH

FOR SADIE AND THE KINGS HOUSE HOTEL

OSCAR AND ARABELLA: HOT HOT HOT
by Neal Layton

British Library Cataloguing in Publication Data
A catalogue record of this book is available from
the British Library.
ISBN 0 340 87326 4 (HB)

First edition published 2003
10 9 8 7 6 5 4 3 2 1

Published by Hodder Children's Books
a division of Hodder Headline Limited
338 Euston Road London NW1 3BH

Printed in Hong Kong

Oscar and Arabella HOT HOT HOT

by Neal Layton

Hodder
Children's
Books

A division of Hodder Headline Limited

Oscar was a woolly mammoth.
And so was Arabella.

They lived a long time ago in
a time called the ice age.

For most of the year it was winter.
Oscar and Arabella liked the winter.

They liked the snow, the ice and the freezing arctic winds.

But then summer
would arrive.

Oscar and Arabella
didn't like the
summer.

The sun would come out and melt all the ice and snow. Thousands of brightly coloured plants would appear from the ground, irritating their eyes and trunks.

'ATCHOO!

Then there were the insects...

And the dust.
And this summer was worse than most.

Buzzzzzzz

There didn't seem to be any end in sight, it just seemed to be getting hotter **and hotter** and hotter.

Oscar found a last piece
of ice behind a rock.

But as soon as he took it into
the sun it disappeared.

And still it got **hotter**.

Arabella suggested that they seek shelter under the trees.

But none of the trees were big enough.
And it got hotter still.

Oscar thought he could
fan Arabella with a big leaf.

It kept Arabella cool but made him even hotter than he had been before.

Arabella suggested
that if they jumped
in the lake it might
help cool them down
a bit.

PLOSH!!

But that didn't
work either.

There was only one solution.

They would have to give each other a HAIR CUT!

It was drastic, but it worked.

At last they felt cool!

When all the other animals saw them,
they decided to do the same.

The new fashion seemed to suit some animals more than others but at least now everybody was happy.

And thankfully,
summer never
lasts forever.

The world turned on
its axis, winter
set in once more...
and all the animals
grew back their
woolly coats.

Well almost all the animals...

ICE AGE FACTS

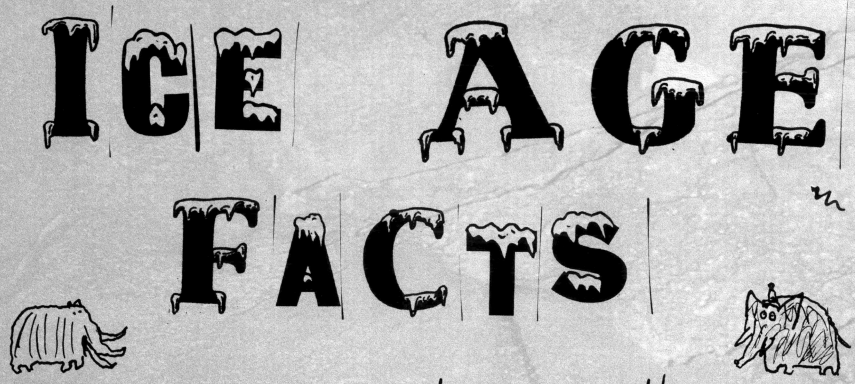

There ~~has~~ has actually been more than one ice age. Oscar and Arabella would ~~have~~ have lived in the most recent one which ended about 10,000 years ago.

They had seasons in the ICE AGE much like ours though their summers would have been much shorter.

They probably didn't have combs, mirrors or scissors in the ICE AGE I made that bit up. They would have more likely cut their woolly coats with blunt stone axes.

Most scientists think there will be another ICE AGE in a few thousand thousand years...